San Jose, CA

Hammer

TAMALE QUILT

IPE ♦ QUILT PATTERN

To the students of School
Hammer Elem.
May books open worlds
of wonder & magic.
Enjoy!

11-18-98

PB
F
TEN

The Tamale Quilt
Copyright © 1998 Jane Tenorio-Coscarelli
Publisher : 1/4 Inch Designs & Publishing
Copy Editor : Jane Tenorio-Coscarelli
Translation Editor: Nicole Coscarelli
Quilt Designers : Linda Sawrey, Jane Coscarelli
Machine Quilted: Rose Burroughs
Quilt Photography by :Carina Woolrich Photography

Published by
1/4 Inch Designs & Publishing
39165 Silktree Drive
Murrieta Ca. 92563 USA

Library of Congress Cataloging Card Number: 98-91732

ISBN: HB 0-9653422-3-9
       PB 0-9653422-4-7

Printed in Hong Kong

10 9 8 7 6 5 4 3 2 1

To my father
John D. Tenorio
" Pa"
For holding your daughter's hand in
times of trouble.
For the sense of humor you have given me.
And for the memories I will always share
with my children.
To my family and friends who have only
encouraged me along.
To those of you who have opened your
home and heart to my books.
I hope they will rekindle the memories
you hold dear.
A heartfelt thank you
Enjoy
Janie

" Mija, God gave you a gift, you need to use it"
-Nana

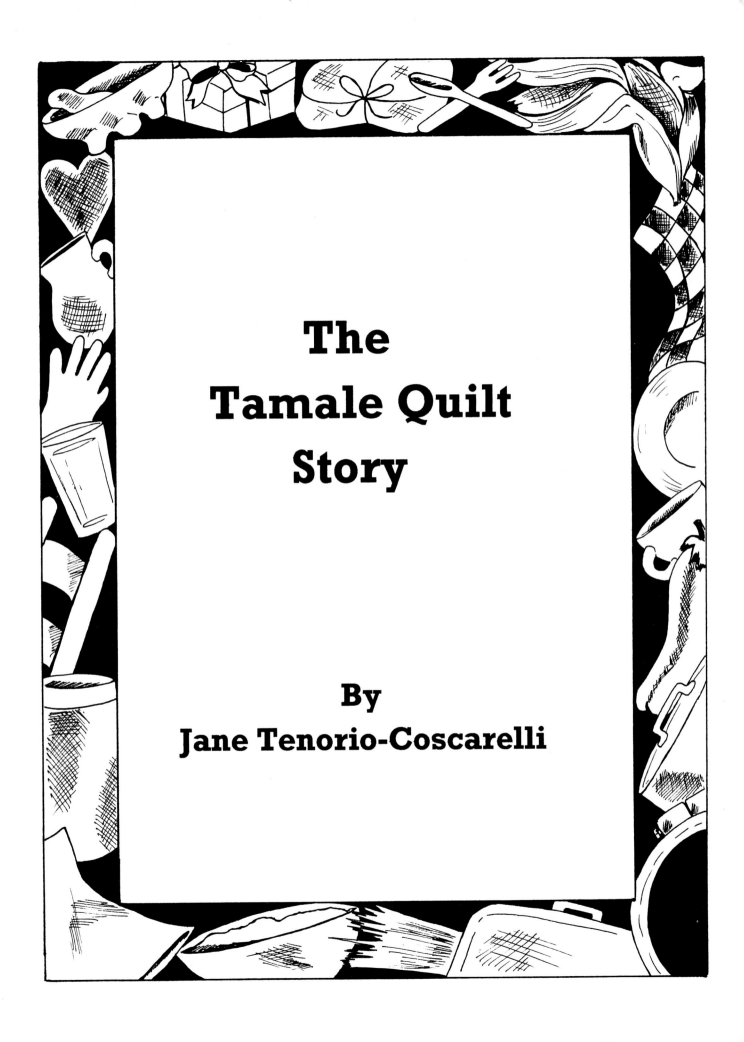

The Tamale Quilt Story

By
Jane Tenorio-Coscarelli

Rosa waited impatiently under the blankets that covered her,

adjusting the pillows as the minutes passed.

The disappointment of being sick for the **holiday season** showed
                                            las Navidades
on her face. She heard the **door** open, and felt the chilled air that
                            puerta
announced Nana Isabel's arrival. Her little brother Manuel

greeted their **grandmother** at the door with big **hugs** and **kisses**.
              abuela   *abrazos*   *besos*
"Nana! Nana!" he yelled.

"Oh! Nana I am so **happy** to see you," Rosa's soft weak voice
                   alegre
called out from the couch.

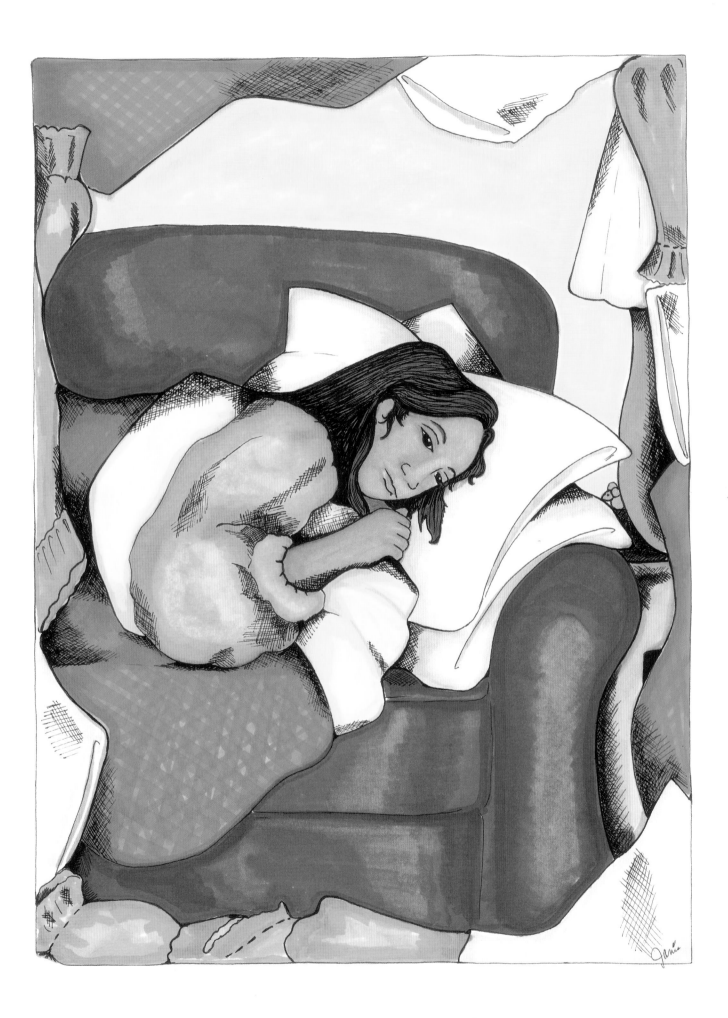

Nana walked over to Rosa and kissed her forehead.

"How is my precious angel feeling **today**?" Nana asked.
hoy

"**Better**." whispered Rosa.
Mejor

Nana smiled "You will be better **soon**" she whispered.
pronto

Reaching down for little Manuel's hand she said.

"Come Manuel, help me **unpack**. In my old
desempacar

brown suitcase I have brought a story to share."
maleta marrona

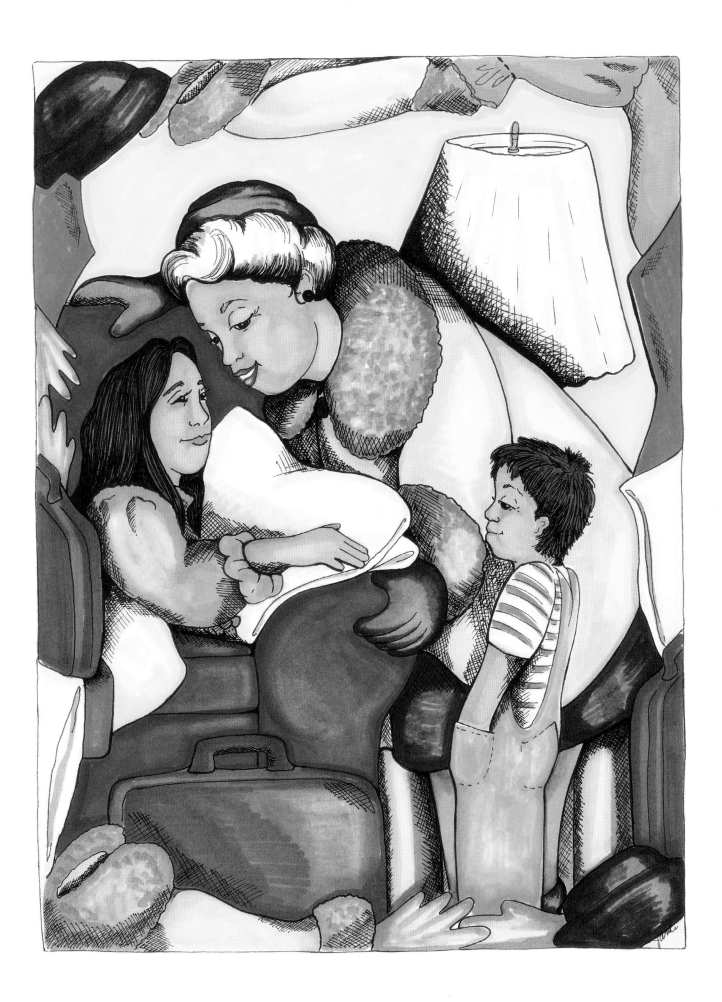

Soon **evening** came. Nana walked to the couch where Rosa laid.
noche

"We finally finished unpacking," announced Nana.

"Yes, finally," the tired Manuel said.

Tucked under Nana's arm was a quilt. Manuel climbed up on

the couch to **sit** next to his sister. As she unfolded the quilt
sentarse
Nana said "I want to tell you the **story** of my Tamale quilt."
cuento
"The Tamale quilt," Manuel and Rosa repeated, giggling as they

looked at each other with puzzled expressions.

Nana just smiled and began her story.

"When I was a little **girl** growing up on my father's **farm,**
                                 niña   *granja*
each year my **mother** would make tamales.
                        madre
I would sit on the big **red** can of lard in the middle of the
                               roja
kitchen, where I could reach the bowl of olives that were on the

table.

My little **brother** Juan would stand right next to me because he
               hermano
was too small to sit and reach across the table for the olives.

I would watch as my mother **crushed** the dry **corn** in her
                             machacar   *maiz*
stone bowl to make cornmeal for the masa. Mother would
 molcajete
mix the other dry **ingredients** together. Then she would
mezclar   *ingredientes*
add the lard, blending it in slowly.

The masa would get so **big** and heavy that my **father** would
                                    grande   *padre*
come from the field to help. **Rolling up his sleeves**, he would
                                      arrenmangarse
start to **knead** the masa. We would tell **stories** and **laugh**
                amasar   *cuentos*   *reirse*
together in our little **kitchen.**
                        cocina

16

My mother would take a small **ball** of masa and **drop** it into
bola *echar*
a **large** glass of **water**. If it floated to the **top** of the glass, it
vaso *agua* *lo alto*
was ready to spread on the corn leaves.

Juan and I would dry the **corn husks** that had been **soaking**
                   envoltura de la mazorca   *remojandose*
in **water**, and lay them **flat**. Then mother would **spread**
    agua   *plano*   *untar*
the masa onto the **husks** with her **wooden spoon**. Next
                   envolturas   *cuchara de madera*
she would add the **chili sauce** and then we would add
                   salsa de chile
the **olive** in the **middle** of the tamale. This was our favorite
    aceituna   *medio*   *favorito*
part because we could **eat** the extra olives.
                   comer

Mother would then fold the tamales into a **little package**
                                                paquete pequeno
and set them in a **big kettle** on the **stove** to cook. I would
                olla grande   *estufa*
help my mother **clean up** when we were done in the
                    limpiar
kitchen. While the tamales cooked, they filled the house with
cocina
the smell of masa and chili.

My whole family would get **dressed** up to go to **midnight** mass
        vestirse   *medianoche*
Mother would always pack a **dozen** of her homemade tamales
          docena
to give to the **church**.
     iglesia

It was Christmas **morning** when we **returned** home from
                     mañana   *volieron*
church. My Mother would make **hot chocolate** to warm us up,
                               chocolate caliente
and serve her **delicious** fresh tamales. It didn't take long for us
                 deliciosos
to finish eating every bite of our tamales.

Then the whole family would **sing** Christmas **carols** while we
                           cantar   *villancicos*
opened our presents.

After opening presents with full tummies, it was time for **bed.**

cama

My brother and I would slowly crawl into our warm beds and

wait for Mother and Father to tuck us in.

We would **dream** of the **holiday** we shared together and of

soñar   *diafestivo*

Mother's special chocolate and tamale **supper.**

cena

As I grew up, I learned to cook and to sew. I would **make** my
hacer

Mother's tamales for the holidays and sew quilts for special

people in my life. One year I decided to make my mother a

special **gift** to open on Christmas Eve by combining her tamales
regalo

with one of my quilts.

And that is how the Tamale Quilt came to be," Nana added.

"Now listen closely and I will tell you about the **colors** I picked
colores

and the **pattern** of the quilt".
dibujo

The **red flowers** and **hearts** were for the **chile sauce** cooking
　　flores rojas　　*corazones*　　　*salsa de chile*
on my mother's stove. The **smell** of love would fill the **whole**
　　　　　　　　　　olor　　　　　　　　　*toda*
house.　The **green leaves** were the **fields** of corn that my brother
　　　　hojas verdes　　　*campos*
and I **played** hide-and-seek in as **children.** We also
　　jugaron　　　　　　*niños*
helped **harvest** and dry the corn to make the meal for masa.
　　cosechar

The **yellow** was the corn **husk**, that we dried and **wrapped** up
    amarillo   *envoltura*   *envolveiron*
with masa and chili, and that mother folded into little tamale

presents which cooked on the stove.

The **brown hands** are my mother's and father's hands as they
    manos morenas
kneaded the heavy masa, until it **floated** to the top of the **glass**.
                              floto   *vaso*

The **black circles** are my favorite olives, a **little surprise** in
  circulos negros   *pequeña sorpresa*
the **middle** of each tamale. I remember how my brother and I
  medio
would eat the leftover ones when we were finished **cooking.**
                                                    cocinando

As Nana finished her story Rosa fell **asleep** under the
                              dormida
tamale quilt, warmed from her heart to her toes by Nana's

memories of the **farm** . Tucking the quilt tightly around her,
recuerdos   ***granja***
Nana **kissed** Rosa **goodnight** .
     besar   ***buenas noches***
"Come on Manuel, we will go help your mother with her

tamales and let your **sister** sleep." Nana said taking his hand.
     hermana
Quietly they both walked into the **kitchen** to help.
     cocina

38

Days passed, and Nana began to pack her brown suitcase to

return home.

Feeling much better, Rosa came into Nana's room holding the
Sentiendo
tamale quilt.

"Here Nana don't forget the Tamale quilt," Rosa reminded her.

Nana stopped packing, put her **hand** on Rosa's shoulder and
mano
said "The tamale quilt is yours now and the stories are now

yours to tell. Someday you can share them with your **children**."
niños
Nana smiled.

"Oh thank you Nana! Thank you!" Rosa said, hugging her quilt

Smiling at her Nana, Rosa wrapped the quilt around herself.

She knew that the tamale quilt would always **wrap** her in love
envolver
for **years** to come. And that made her feel much better from her
años
heart to her **toes.**
dedos
THE END
40

DID YOU
FIND
THE MOUSE
ON EACH
PAGE?

TAMALES

Note: Tamales can be filled with meat, vegetables, cheese, or fruit.
This recipe is for meat filled tamales

Masa Recipe Corn Meal Tamales

Makes two dozen tamales

1 1/2 pounds Lard

5 teaspoons baking powder

Salt to taste

5 pounds masa cornmeal

(Purchase masa cornmeal from a Mexican store)

With spoon whip lard until consistency of whipping cream.

Sift together baking soda, salt and masa, add to lard.

Beat until fluffy

Testing: Make a small ball of masa. Drop into a glass of water.

If it floats to the top of glass it is ready.

Note: If masa seems too dry, you can add a little of the broth from meat
filling to masa. Do not add too much because it will make tamales mushy.

Corn Husks

24- Corn Husk Leaves (Two husks per tamale)

Soak husks in warm water for about 1 hour, until soft and bendable.

Drain water and lightly dry husks.

Take two husks and lay them side by side, overlapping the sides.

Using a wooden spoon spread about a spoonful of masa onto husk.

Covering only the center of the husk, not the ends.

Add a spoon full of red chile filling.

Add black olive in center.

Fold husk sides in. Then fold top and bottom of husks to make package.

Place in a streamer and cover.

Cook about 1 hour until masa is no longer doughy.

Cool, unwrapped and serve.

Red Chile Sauce - Meat Filling

The following filling recipe can use either beef, pork or chicken for meat.

2- 28 oz.. Cans Red Chile Sauce   **3 Pounds Boiled Shredded Meat**

7- Tablespoons flour   **(Pork, Beef or Chicken)**

Garlic powder   **Salt**

1-small can Pitted Black Olives

Cook meat in kettle with two onions. Add garlic powder and salt to taste.

Boil until meat can be shredded. Drain

Add chile sauce to kettle, adding flour to thicken mixture.

THE TAMALE QUILT

58" x 58"
Designed by
Linda Sawrey & Jane Tenorio-Coscarelli

The Tamale Quilt

Quilt size 58"x58"   9 Blocks -each-12" Finished

Materials

3 yds- Light background & border fabric

9 -1/4 yds - 9 different fabrics for T-block (2 1/4 yds total)

        2- Blues

        2- Reds

        2- Golds

        2- Greens

        1- Tan

1 1/2 yds- Lattice & Binding fabric

2 3/4 yds- Backing fabric

60"x 60" Batting

Note: Cutting uses rotary cutting method. Piecing uses 1/4" seam allowance.

1. Cut & piece 36 T-units pieces #1 & #2. Cutting directions are for 36 T-units to make 9-12" completed T blocks.

Cutting Table

Piece	Fabrics	# of Pieces	Dimensions	
#1	Background	18	4 7/8" x 4 7/8"	
#1	Each T- fabric	2	4 7/8" x 4 7/8"	
	using 9 different fabric			
#2	Background	45	2 7/8" x 2 7/8"	
#2	Every T- colored fabric	5	2 7/8" x 2 7/8"	
	9 Different fabrics			

You get 4 T-units from each of the 9 different colored fabrics.

2. Piecing sequence for T- unit

T-units make 36
Finished size 6"x6"

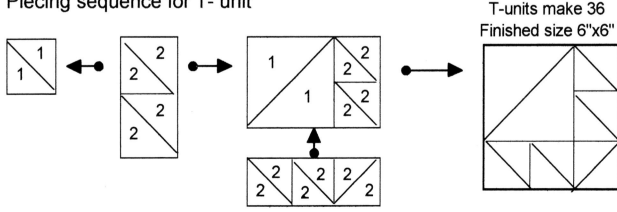

3. Piece 4 different T-units together.
   Press. Complete to 12" finished block.
   Make 9

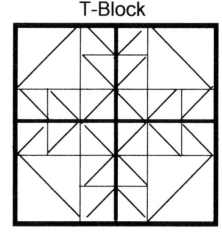
T-Block

Lattice & Cornerstones

4. Cut 24- 3"X12 1/2" lattice strip fabric.
   Cut 16- 3" cornerstone fabric.
   Sew lattice strips to each side of
   T blocks in a three blocks row. Repeat three times for 9 blocks

 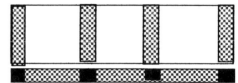

Sew 3 lattice strips 4 cornerstones together alternating each.
Make four complete strips. Line up seams, pin in place at seams.
Sew to top and bottom of block rows.
Refer to photo for placement. Press

Borders

6. Cut 2 borders 6 1/2" X 46"
   (approximate length and adjust
   to your quilt top)
   Sew to top and bottom of quilt
   top. Press
7. Cut 2 borders 6 1/2" x 58"
   (approximate as above) Sew to
   sides of quilt top. Press
8. Trace applique pieces. Appliqué
   onto borders. Press. Remember
   to add seam allowance to
   appliqué templates.

Finishing

9. Layer backing, batting and quilt top.
   Baste in place. Hand or machine quilt.
   (Refer to basic quilt book for directions if needed.)
   Bind using any method you prefer.